Puffin Books

Singenpoo
Strikes
Again

Major Mac pointed straight at me.
'There he is,' he growled.
'There's the one who stole my cat.'

Mac the two-legged rat is back.
And Singenpoo* is in trouble...

More claws, cliffhangers and
crackpots from the mad mind
of Paul Jennings.

* Singenpoo is a weird name. But then
Singenpoo is a weird cat. You can read
more about her in *The Paw Thing*.

Other books by Paul Jennings

Unreal!
Unbelievable!
Quirky Tails
Uncanny!
Unbearable!
Unmentionable!
Undone!
Uncovered!
Round the Twist

The Cabbage Patch Fib
The Cabbage Patch War
(illustrated by Craig Smith)

The Paw Thing
(illustrated by Keith McEwan)

The Gizmo
The Gizmo Again
Come Back Gizmo
Sink the Gizmo
(illustrated by Keith McEwan)

Wicked!
(with Morris Gleitzman)

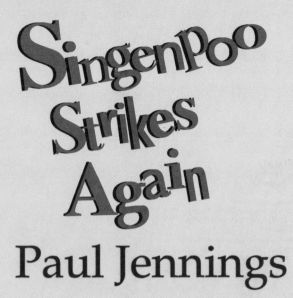

Singenpoo Strikes Again

Paul Jennings

Illustrated by
Keith McEwan

PUFFIN BOOKS

Puffin Books
Penguin Books Australia Ltd
487 Maroondah Highway, PO Box 257
Ringwood, Victoria 3134, Australia
Penguin Books Ltd
Harmondsworth, Middlesex, England
Viking Penguin, A Division of Penguin Books USA Inc.
375 Hudson Street, New York, New York 10014, USA
Penguin Books Canada Limited
10 Alcorn Avenue, Toronto, Ontario, Canada M4V 3B2
Penguin Books (N.Z.) Ltd
Cnr Rosedale and Airborne Roads, Albany, New Zealand

First published by Penguin Books Australia, 1998
10 9 8 7 6 5 4 3 2 1
Copyright © Greenleaves Pty Ltd, 1998
Illustrations Copyright © Keith McEwan, 1998

Typeset in 12½/15pt Palatino by Midland Typesetters, Maryborough, Victoria
Made and printed in Australia by Australian Print Group, Maryborough, Victoria

National Library of Australia
Cataloguing-in-Publication data:

Jennings, Paul, 1943– .
Singenpoo strikes again

ISBN 0 14 130099 X

I. McEwan, Keith. II. Title.

A823.3

To Jasmin Synnøve
  Keith

I can hardly bear to write about it.

Poor old Singenpoo. After herding all the mice out of Major Mac's chicken shop like a sheepdog you'd think everything would have been great. But no. It was worse than ever. Major Mac had promised to treat the cat like a queen. And he did for a week or two. But now he was mean to the poor thing again. He never patted her. He didn't even feed her properly. All she got was beaks and claws like before.

Last year, he believed that Singenpoo could read. But now he'd changed his mind. He sure had a short memory – when it suited him.

'Don't be stupid,' he said. 'A cat couldn't read a book about sheepdogs. Cats are dumb. Cats are stupid. And this one is worse than average.'

I knew Singenpoo could read but I had to keep quiet or Mac would get mad with me. He might even decide to have Singenpoo put down like before. So I just swept up the floor of his take-away chicken shop, put out the rubbish bins and served the customers as usual. I didn't want to get the sack. I needed the money. After-school jobs were hard to get.

You'd have thought that he'd have been glad to have a cat like Singenpoo. I mean, a lot of kids came into that shop just to see her read.

I used to put three or four big pieces of cardboard on the floor. Each one had a word written on it. 'Point to RABBIT,' I would say. Singenpoo could walk straight over and put her paw on the correct word.

All the kids in the shop clapped and cheered and I gave Singenpoo a bit of chicken as a reward.

Singenpoo could point to lots of words – TREE, CAT, CHICKEN, BIRD, COW and HOG. Her favourites were CAT and CHICKEN. She always started purring if you asked for them. She hated DOG. If you said DOG she would walk up and down with her hair all fluffed up and then run off.

There was no way she would ever read the word DOG or even go near it.

Every night after work, Mac closed up the shop and sat on his favourite chair. Then he would get his glass of wine and watch me sweep the floor. He used to open the wine at lunchtime and leave a glass of it in the storeroom to 'breathe'. He thought it tasted better that way.

While I was sweeping he would give orders. 'You missed a bit,' he would yell. 'What's wrong with you? Is something wrong with your eyes? Look – here and here and here.' He would run his finger over the floor and show me the dust that I had missed.

'You're useless,' he would shout. 'As bad as the stupid cat.'

One night he was in a really bad mood. He had been complaining all day. The food was bad. The weather was bad. The customers were mean. He sipped at his wine and pulled a sour face. 'This stuff gets worse every day,' he said. 'I don't know what's the matter with it. They just don't make it like they used to.' He turned his attention to me and Singenpoo. 'I'm going to get rid of that cat,' he said. 'It's got fleas.'

'Last time you got rid of her,' I said, 'Singenpoo saved you from a mouse plague.'

'The mice all ran off,' said Mac. 'The cat had nothing to do with it.'

He had a convenient memory when he was in a bad mood. I tried to think of something to cheer him up.

'Look,' I said. I took out Singenpoo's words and a clean piece of cardboard. On it I wrote the words MAJOR MAC in big letters. 'She can even read your name,' I said.

Mac gave a small grin. He liked the idea of a cat being able to read his name. 'Okay, Singenpoo,' I said. 'Point to Major Mac.'

Singenpoo walked up and down the row of words. She looked at HOG, she looked at TREE, and she looked at COW. Finally she stopped at MAJOR MAC. I gave a grin. So did Mac.

Singenpoo stepped onto the piece of cardboard and squatted. Then she did a pee. All over Mac's name. Yellow cat's pee ran all over the words and joined them together in a big blur. Mac was furious.

He grabbed hold of Singenpoo with one hand.
'Oh no,' I said to myself. 'He's going to have her
put down.' I just couldn't stand the thought of
life without Singenpoo. But it was all right. He
took her into the storeroom and locked the door.
Then he plonked himself on his favourite chair.

'Where's my wine?' he said.

'You took it into the storeroom with you,' I
said. Mac went back and opened the storeroom
door a fraction and Singenpoo shot out.

She raced across the room straight into the leg of a chair. Singenpoo staggered around like a ...

'Drunk,' yelled Mac. He sniffed Singenpoo. 'The silly cat smells of wine,' he roared. 'It's been sipping my wine. Get it out of here. It's fired. It's sacked. I never want to see it again.'

'Can I have her?' I asked.

'I don't care what you do with it,' shouted Mac. 'Just get rid of it.'

I was rapt. I grabbed Singenpoo and ran all the way home without stopping. Mac had given her to me. She was my cat. She was safe for ever.

2

At home things were good. But at work they got worse and worse. Mac yelled and shouted. Once I gave a customer the wrong change. I handed her a twenty dollar note instead of a ten. Mac was furious. He docked ten dollars off my pay. Two hours work. Sweeping and serving. All for nothing. And it wasn't as if I was well paid. Five dollars an hour was chicken feed.

Then I finally found out what was wrong. Why I missed some of the dust. And gave the wrong change. And kept bumping into things.

I couldn't see properly.

Mum took me to see Mr Spock, the optometrist. 'You're going to have to wear glasses,' he said in a kind voice.

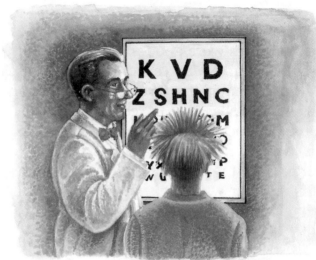

That wasn't so bad in itself. Lots of people wear glasses. And I was glad that I was able to see letters and words properly. The only trouble was, the glasses kept steaming up at work. Whenever I was cooking chicken the fumes would make my glasses fog up so I still couldn't see what I was doing.

One night the place was packed out and I was working like crazy. Someone ordered the Family Special. Fifteen pieces of chicken with barbecue sauce, four large buckets of chips, and four chocolate thick shakes. 'Hurry it up,' yelled Mac. 'Hurry it up, idiot.'

My glasses were really fogging up and I had to keep stopping to clean them. Every time I did Mac would yell at me.

I staggered out of the kitchen and gave the customers their Family Special. Everything was okay for about two minutes and then they started to yell and scream and spit. One guy was being sick in the corner.

'Urgh,' he yelled. 'There's barbecue sauce in the thick shake and chocolate on the chicken.'

'Jeez, sorry,' I said to Mac. 'But you wouldn't let me stop to clean my glasses. I couldn't see.'

Mac went red in the face. He started to shout. 'You're sacked too,' he screamed. 'Get out and don't come back.'

Boy, I was mad. I was sick of him. 'Don't worry,' I yelled back. 'I wouldn't work here if you paid me.'

I walked home sad and angry. Mum was going to be upset. She was on the pension and we didn't have much money. My dad had left home years ago and we were all on our own. Just me and Mum. And Singenpoo.

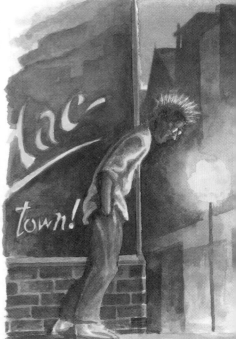

Days and weeks and months went by. I checked the papers and went looking for jobs. But no one had any vacancies. Part-time work was really hard to get.

So I used the time to teach Singenpoo more words. She tried really hard. Just to please me. She felt sorry for me. Singenpoo was my best friend. I would do anything for her and she would do anything for me.

Then something happened. Something I had never expected. I couldn't believe my eyes. I was reading the comics in the paper one day when a photo caught my eye. It was a picture of a dog. A dog pointing to a word written on a blackboard.

Underneath it said, THE WORLD'S SMARTEST DOG.

My eyes grew round as I read the story. This dog called Mungo could read words. Every time its master said a word Mungo pointed to it on the blackboard.

'Listen to this,' I said to Mum. I read it out aloud.

' "Mr Gerald Cane of Adelaide has a dog that can point to words. During one trial Mungo pointed to the words RAT, TIN, MAN and PEG. Mungo has been on television and now performs daily at shows throughout the country. Mr Cane has grown rich on Mungo's earnings." '

Wow,' I yelled. 'They're really easy words. Singenpoo can read better than that. Yesterday she pointed to CONSTIPATION. You can't get much harder than that.'

This was wonderful news. If people paid to go and see Mungo, they would pay to see Singenpoo.

We were going to be rich.

3

The next night there was a knock on the door. I couldn't believe it. Standing there as large as life was Major Mac. And next to him was a cop. Major Mac pointed straight at me. 'There he is,' he growled. 'There's the one who stole my cat.'

'You gave her to me,' I yelled. 'She's mine.'

Mac leered at me. 'Get real,' he said. 'I wouldn't give away a valuable animal like that. Not a cat that can read.'

What a rat. Mac was such a liar. I looked at Mum.

She took a deep breath. 'Scott is a very honest boy,' she said firmly. 'He would never steal anything.'

'Oh no?' said Mac. 'What about the time he gave away ten of my dollars?'

Mum's eyes narrowed. 'That was an honest mistake,' she said. 'Scott needed glasses. He couldn't see the notes properly. Don't you call my boy a thief. If he says you gave him the cat, then I believe him. Why don't you get lost?'

My mum had guts. I was real proud of her. I took a step towards Mac. 'Yeah,' I said. 'No one pushes us around.'

Mac's face started to turn purple. He wasn't used to being talked to like that. He turned to the cop. 'Arrest that boy,' he shouted. 'He stole my cat.'

The cop looked sad. I could tell that he felt sorry for me. 'Can you prove that Major Mac gave you the cat?' he said to me.

I shook my head.

'Yeah,' said Mac. 'Prove it. Show me a receipt. Everyone knows it's my cat. It's been at the chicken shop for years. I've been training it to read. And this lazy kid, Scott, pinches it.'

This was terrible. Mac was lying his head off. 'I taught her to read,' I shouted. 'And he gave her to me.' I could feel tears welling up in my eyes. Mum put her arms around my shoulders and tried to calm me down.

'Here, pussy,' said Mac. 'Come to Daddy.' Singenpoo cringed and ran under the sofa. She wouldn't come out.

Mac scowled. 'The kid's turned it against me,' he said. 'That cat used to love me.'

The cop spoke to Mum. 'Look, I'm sorry,' he said. 'But you'll have to give the cat back if you can't prove she was a present. Otherwise I will have to charge you and the case will go to court.'

Mum put a hand on my shoulder. 'Go and get her, Scott,' said Mum. 'We can't afford to go to court. You'll have to give Singenpoo back.'

I shook my head. 'Never,' I yelled. 'Never.'

Mum reached under the sofa. She pulled out the trembling cat and put her in Mac's big hairy arms. Singenpoo meowed terribly. She was shivering and frightened. She didn't want to go back to Mac. But he held her tight and walked back to his car.

'Sorry,' said the cop. 'I'm really sorry.'

I ran down the hall and threw myself onto the bed. I started punching the pillow. I pretended it was Mac's face. Jeez, I was mad. Everything was going wrong. We had lost our chance to make a fortune. And even worse – my lovely cat Singenpoo was back with Mac. I gave the pillow an extra-hard punch. 'Take that, you rat,' I shouted.

4

I'd almost given up looking for a job. My heart just wasn't in it. Singenpoo had gone. Back to Mac's horrible shop. Back to starvation. Back to meanness and neglect.

One night I snuck up to the chicken shop to see if I could catch sight of Singenpoo. I stared through the window. There was no sign of her.

But there was another sign. A big one stuck up on the door.

PET READING COMPETITION

MUNGO THE DOG

— **VS.** —

SINGENPOO THE CAT

Great Readathon!

TICKETS $20.00

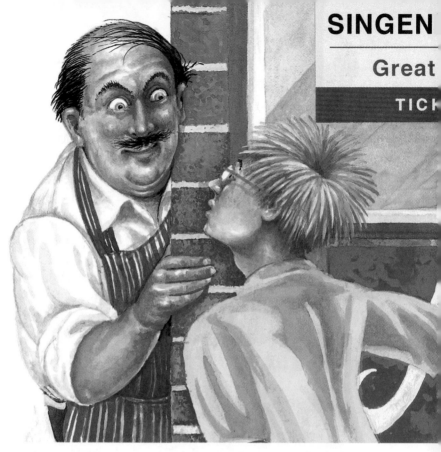

What? Mac was entering Singenpoo in a competition against Mungo the dog. I couldn't believe it.

'Ah, Scott,' said a voice. It was Mac. He had seen me. 'I've been looking for you.'

I stared up at him. He was trying to be friendly. He was actually talking to me in a kind voice.

'What's going on?' I said. 'What are you doing to Singenpoo?'

'Nothing,' he said in a sickly sweet tone. 'Just a little chance to make some money. If the rotten ... er ... lovely little pussy wins.'

'Singenpoo could beat that dog easy,' I yelled. 'You'll be rich.'

'How would you like your job back?' said Mac in an oily voice. 'How would you like to be in on it?'

'Why?' I said. 'What do you want me for?'

I was just about to spit in his face. I was just about to tell him what I thought of him. But then I started to think about Mum and how broke she was. And Singenpoo. It would give me a chance to see her again. I didn't have any choice.

I choked back all the words that I really wanted to say and nodded.

'Good,' said Mac. 'You can start right now.'

Mac took me into the back of the shop. 'Where's Singenpoo?' I asked.

'In there,' said Mac. He pointed to the storeroom. There was a big padlock on the door. 'Rotten thing keeps trying to run away,' he said.

He unlocked the door. I looked inside. There was Mac's open bottle. There was his glass of wine breathing on the shelf. But where was Singenpoo?

Something hit me in the face like a gust of wind in a storm. Something soft and warm and scared. It was Singenpoo. She was so glad to see me. She wrapped her poor paws around my neck and started to purr. Then she saw Mac and began to hiss.

Mac backed away. 'It won't come near me,' he growled. 'Won't do a thing I say. Or anyone else for that matter.'

5

So that was it. Singenpoo wouldn't do what Mac wanted. He couldn't get her to point to the words. She would only do it for me. That's why he wanted me back. What a ratbag. He was using me. And I had no choice but to go along with it.

Mac tried to reach out for Singenpoo but she saw him coming and jumped out of my arms. She shot across the floor and ran straight into the broom. She staggered around the room. The poor thing. Mac grabbed her and sniffed her fur. 'It's been at my wine again,' he said. 'Drunk as a lord.'

I took Singenpoo from his hands and sniffed. She did smell of wine. There was no doubt about that. Mac fetched his glass and took a sip. He pulled a face. 'Keep it away from my grog,' he said. 'It'll never win if it drinks.
And it'll be your fault.
You're in charge.'

'Of what?' I said.

Mac grabbed my shoulder. 'Look,' he growled. 'There's going to be a big show. Mungo the dog is going to be there. And this stupid cat. There will be a big audience. And the TV people are coming. The winner gets all the door money. The loser gets nothing.'

'And you want me to get Singenpoo to point to words?'

Mac nodded.

'What's in it for me?' I said.

'What do you want?' growled Mac.

'Singenpoo,' I said. 'And five hundred dollars for Mum. You can keep the rest.'

Mac thought about it for a minute. Then he gave a sly sort of grin and held out his hand. 'It's a deal,' he said. 'You get the cat plus five hundred bucks.'

'Promise?' I said.

'Promise,' said Mac.

Every day I went to the shop and taught Singenpoo new words. She was much happier than before. She purred a lot and her coat was shiny and thick. She was glad to have me back. There was no doubt about that.

And she was really keen to learn new words. There were hundreds and hundreds all written in big letters on sheets of cardboard. Sometimes she would make mistakes – especially if I scribbled. But mostly she got them right.

On the first day Mac went into the storeroom and fetched his open bottle of wine. Then he poured a glass and watched me.

I looked at the row of words on the floor. 'Dinosaur,' I said. Singenpoo walked over and put her paw on the right card.

'Good girl,' I said.

Mac took a sip of his sour wine and put down his glass. 'Keep the cat away from this,' he said. 'If it gets over .05 it won't be able to read properly.'

Mac slammed the door and went out. I was alone in the shop. I grabbed a texta and put a little mark on the side of his glass to show the level of the wine. I had to find out if Singenpoo was really drinking it.

It took me about an hour to sweep up the shop. I knew that Mac would be back at any time so I checked the level of the wine in his glass. The level had changed. 'Oh no,' I said. 'Singenpoo, you shouldn't have.' But I couldn't help laughing.

7

The big day finally came. And we had prepared well. In my bedroom I had hundreds and hundreds of words written in big, black letters. Singenpoo could point to them all. Some of them were really long ones. Mungo wouldn't have a chance. I was sure of it. Mac would get the money. And Singenpoo would be mine.

The competition was in a huge room at the university. All the people sat in rows of seats that stretched up in front of the stage. There were bright lights and TV cameras. There were thousands of people. And each one had paid twenty dollars to get in.

Singenpoo was in a small cage. 'Just to make sure she doesn't nick off,' said Mac.

Suddenly I started to worry. What if Mungo knew more words than Singenpoo? Then Mac would keep her. Or worse ...

Mr Cane walked in. He had Mungo, an ugly bulldog, on a lead. Singenpoo started to meow and crouch down in her cage. Mungo growled – he didn't like cats at all.

'Quiet, boy. Sit,' said Mr Cane. Mungo sat down straight away. It was a smart dog. A very smart dog.

Mum was in the front row sitting next to the kids who used to watch Singenpoo in the chicken shop. At least we had a few supporters there. Also in the front row was someone else that I knew. Mr Spock.

Mac sat nearby biting his fingernails. He looked as worried as me. If Singenpoo won, he would make a lot of money. If not, he would get nothing.

The judge walked up to the microphone. 'Now, folks,' he said. 'I would like to introduce the world's smartest dog. I give you, Mungo the Marvellous.'

A huge roar went up. People stamped and clapped and cheered. Everyone seemed to know Mungo. The dog sat up on his hind legs and begged. The audience laughed. They really liked him.

Singenpoo seemed frightened by all the noise. The judge asked for silence. Then he said, 'And now may I introduce the cat, er ... ' He looked embarrassed. 'Singing Power.'

'Singenpoo,' I said quietly.

There was a big cheer from Mum, and the kids from the chicken shop clapped. But there was just a bit of laughter and polite clapping from the rest of the audience. Mungo was the favourite, I could see that.

'Okay,' said the judge. 'Here are the rules. One hundred words are written on the blackboard. Scott and Mr Cane have half the words each written on cards. They will take it in turns to call out the word on their next card. Their animal will touch that word on the blackboard with a paw. The first animal to get twenty-five words correct will win.'

The blackboard was propped up against the wall so that Singenpoo and Mungo could walk up to it. The words were written in small letters in chalk. This had me a bit worried. Singenpoo was used to cards with words written in big black texta. She hadn't had any practice with a blackboard before.

The judge tossed up a coin and nodded to me. 'Tails,' I said.

The coin fell to the floor and the judge bent down and looked at it. 'Heads,' he said. 'Mungo will start. Quiet please.'

Mr Cane took Mungo off his lead and a hush fell over the room. 'Tree,' he said in a clear voice. Mungo trotted over to the board and put a paw on the word TREE. A huge roar of clapping filled the room.

'Correct,' said the judge.

Now it was our turn. I took Singenpoo out of her cage and placed her on the floor. She scampered out and bumped straight into the microphone stand. She staggered around for a bit. I picked her up and looked at her carefully. 'Are you all right, girl?' I said.

Mac shifted around in his seat and stared at Singenpoo with a furious expression on his face. I knew he was thinking that Singenpoo had been at his wine again.

Singenpoo gave a little purr. She seemed okay. I read out the word on my first card. 'Peg,' I said. Singenpoo looked nervously at Mungo and then walked around staring at the words. Finally she stopped at the word PIG. She tapped it with a paw.

'Wrong,' said the judge. 'The score is Mungo one, Singenpoo none.'

·Tame

·Tean

Tee

·Flea

·Float

There was polite clapping from the audience. Singenpoo's fans and Mum were silent.

Mr Cane called out his next word. 'Fog,' he said. Mungo trotted over and tapped a paw on the word FOG. A big cheer went up.

'Tip,' I said to Singenpoo. The poor cat looked terribly upset. What was wrong? These were cinchy words. She could do them easily at home. Singenpoo walked over to the blackboard. She walked up and down in front of it. Finally she tapped a word. TIN. She had picked the wrong word again.

Mac came over to the stage and gave Singenpoo a shake. Then he sniffed her fur. 'She's been at the grog again,' he said. He shoved Singenpoo into my arms and went back to his seat in a temper.

It was Mungo's turn again. 'Rabbit,' called Mr
Cane. The bulldog tapped a paw on the correct
word.

I looked at the word on my next card. 'Art,'
I said to Singenpoo. She tapped her paw on
ANT.

This was terrible. I picked her up
and stroked her. 'What's the matter,
girl?' I said. 'Aren't you feeling well?
You haven't been drinking. I know
it.' Singenpoo looked up at me. If
only she could talk. 'Come on, girl,'
I said. 'Don't be nervous. Relax. You
can do it. I just know you can.' She
seemed to want to tell me something.

But she couldn't. Cats can't talk.
And that's a fact.

It was time for the next word.
'Magazine,' said Mr Cane.
Mungo got it right again.
The crowd clapped
very loudly.

It was our turn again. 'Carpet,' I said to Singenpoo.

She walked over and paused. Then she tapped the word CAMPING.

My heart sank. There was no way we were going to win. I could see Mac scowling in the front row. 'Drunken mongrel,' he said.

Mum smiled at me from her seat. 'Just do your best,' she called out. 'It doesn't matter whether you win or lose. As long as you try.'

I wasn't sure if she was talking to me or Singenpoo. But either way it did matter. If we lost the competition I lost my cat. And I really wanted Mum to have that five hundred dollars. Still and all – it was nice of her to say it.

8

The competition continued for another three rounds. All with the same result. The judge called out the score. 'Mungo seven. Singenpoo none.'

This was terrible. We were going to lose. What was wrong? What, what, what? Singenpoo looked dizzy and upset. She was staggering around in circles.

Just then I noticed something. Mr Spock was beckoning to me. I jumped down from the stage and he whispered in my ear while Mungo was having his next turn.

I stared at Singenpoo.
Then at the writing
on the board.
'So that's it,'
I said.

I rushed over to Singenpoo and took off my glasses. Then I fixed them on Singenpoo's head by bending the arms behind her ears. 'Try these,' I said. 'The writing is too small for you to read.'

Singenpoo really looked funny wearing glasses, but she started purring. Everybody laughed.

Now maybe she would be able to read the words. Maybe we still had a chance. Just maybe.

I looked at the word on my next card. Or rather I didn't look at the word on my next card. They were just a blur. Now *I* couldn't read them. Nothing was going right.

I raced over to Mum. 'Can I borrow your glasses?' I said. Mum handed me her glasses and I stared through them at the next word on my list.

'Elephant,' I said. Singenpoo walked straight over and dabbed at ELEPHANT.

Mum and Singenpoo's fans in the audience went wild. They stamped and cheered like crazy.

'Dinghy,' said Mr Cane. Mungo walked up and down, staring at the blackboard. In the end he put a paw on the word DOUGH. Everyone was quiet. Mungo had made his first mistake.

lephant

ggplant

xperiment

xpand

xplode

Now it was Singenpoo's turn to show what she was made of. Now that she could see properly she started to get words right. And Mungo began to make errors. The bulldog couldn't read any words with silent letters in them like COMB or KNIFE. Gradually Singenpoo started to catch up.

The judge called out the scores after each round.

'Mungo twelve, Singenpoo five.'

'Mungo sixteen, Singenpoo ten.'

'Mungo twenty, Singenpoo seventeen.'

'Mungo twenty-three, Singenpoo twenty-one.'

And then, finally:

'Mungo twenty-four, Singenpoo twenty-four.'

Singenpoo hadn't made one mistake since she'd had my glasses to help her. After twenty minutes we were up to the big moment. We had gone thirty-one rounds.

Mr Cane read Mungo's next word. 'Cat,' he said.

Mungo walked up to the board slowly. The hairs stood up on the back of his neck. He started to growl and scratch. He didn't want to do it. He knew what the word was but he couldn't bring himself to point to it. He barked and yelped and ran in circles. Then he trotted off, sat down in the corner and put his paws over his eyes. Mungo was refusing to point to the word CAT.

The score was twenty-four words each and it was Singenpoo's turn. If she could point to her next word she would win. But could she read it?

I turned over the card. Oh no, no, no. It couldn't be. My heart sank. Of all the words in the world, why did it have to be this one? It wasn't a hard word but I didn't want to say it. No way. But I had to stick to the rules.

'Dog,' I said.

Singenpoo fluffed up her fur. She started to hiss and spit. She ran around the board like crazy. She didn't want to do it. She hated the word DOG. Never in her whole life had she gone near the word DOG. She was going bananas. But … but … but … She quickly dabbed at the board as if it was red hot. She touched the word DOG with her paw and leapt into my arms.

. Dog

'Mungo twenty-four, Singenpoo twenty-five,' yelled the judge.

The crowd went wild. We had won. Mum jumped up and down like crazy. Mr Spock looked really pleased with himself. The kids from the chicken shop ran onto the stage and gave me huge hugs. Even Mac came up wearing a grin that went from ear to ear.

After a bit the judge settled everyone down and spoke into the microphone. 'I present this cheque for three thousand dollars to Major Mac,' he said.

I picked up Singenpoo. 'And this is my prize,' I told him. I laughed out loud. I had my wonderful cat back. I was going to spoil her for the rest of her life. Treat her like a queen. Give her the best of everything. And we could enter more competitions. We might even become rich.

'Not so fast,' said Mac. 'That's my cat. It's going to earn a lot more than three thousand dollars. It's worth a mint.'

'You gave her to me,' I yelled. 'If she won she was mine. That's what you said.'

'Prove it,' said Mac. 'Where's your receipt?'

A silence fell over the gang. There was no one who had heard Mac promise to give me Singenpoo if we won. I couldn't prove it. Singenpoo jumped out of my arms but I hardly noticed. I looked hopelessly at the audience as they started to file out of the room. I couldn't believe that this was happening to me again. There was nothing anyone could do.

Suddenly the gang from the chicken shop started to cheer. They were going really crazy. Everyone on the stage was wild with delight. Everyone except Mac, that is. He was red in the face. What was going on? I turned around and looked.

There was writing on the bottom of the blackboard. It said:

I BELONG
TO SCOTT.
MAC IS A LIAR.

Singenpoo dusted her paws and dropped the chalk. Then she jumped into my arms. Not only was she a champion reader. She could write as well.

Singenpoo was a fantastic cat. And now she was mine for ever.

Mac ran outside to be sick. I couldn't work out why. Until I read the last bit, written in very small letters at the bottom:

P.S. I PEED IN THE WINE.

A word from Paul

When I write a book I always become the main person in the story. But in this yarn the main character is a cat. I really had to scratch my head to figure out what a cat makes of the world.

Cats are smart. They know who you are. They know when its tea-time. But do they really love you? When they rub up against your leg are they just having a bit of a scratch or are they telling you that they care?

Can a cat think? Are there cats in heaven? Does a cat know its name? Why do cats jump onto the laps of people who don't like them? Could a cat read?

In the end it didn't really matter what the answers were. I just made Singenpoo the way I wanted her to be. That's one of the good things about being a writer. You can do what you like.

Cheers

Paul

Mice, madness and mayhem

PAUL JENNINGS

The Paw Thing

Illustrated by
Keith McEwan

Don't miss
the first
SINGENPOO
story